THE WHEEZEWHOMP

JULES BURKE

Cover design and illustrations by LeeAnn Mick
Hardback ISBN-13: **978-1-7366191-0-0**
Paperback ISBN-13: **978-1-7366191-1-7**
eBook ISBN-13: **978-1-7366191-2-4**

Library of Congress Control Number: **2021902600**

DEDICATION

This book is dedicated to my two Wheezewhomps,
Max and Ollie.

The Wheezewhomp sang as the moon skimmed over the mountains. His melody and the moonlight entwined in a rainbow of color and sound above the Valley of Strangers.

\ \ | / /

"Mom, do I look like the Wheezewhomp?"
the little boy asked, just as he did every
night when the song rose from the valley.

"Maybe. No one knows what the
Wheezewhomp looks like. No one has ever
seen him; you know that."

"But, we can hear him. He must be very
beautiful. Just like his song,"
the boy said.

/ / | \ \

He wondered, *Could I be a Wheezewhomp?*
He hummed along to the enchanting music
and dreamed of being a Wheezewhomp.

"Mom, tell me the story of the Wheezewhomp."
With a sigh, his mother began the tale, as she did every night before bed.

"Long before you were born, the Valley of Strangers was an extremely unfriendly place. As you know, every creature in the valley is stunningly strange."

"Some look strange. Some act strange. Some *smell* strange. They speak strange languages and make strange noises too.

The creatures were so afraid of one another that they lived in isolation, even though they felt sad and lonely all the time."

"Everyone in the Valley of Strangers had a job to do, and they did it alone. They ate lunch alone and went home alone.

They only played games that they could play alone. After supper, they went to bed alone, for they all lived alone."

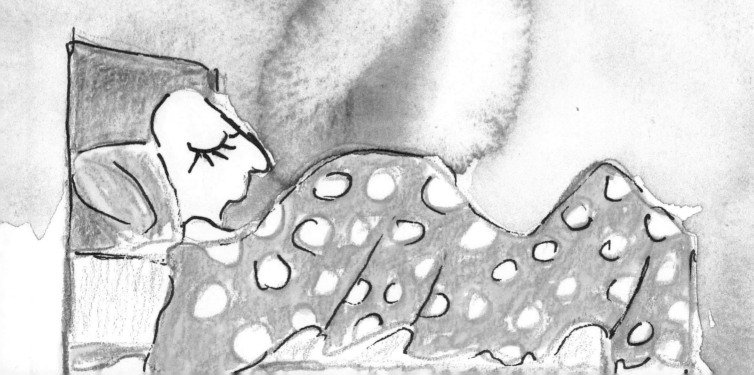

"When one passed by another, they averted their eyes and never spoke. They never fought nor argued. The poor and lonely creatures lived in silence and sadness."

\\ / /

"One warm summer evening, at sunset,
the Wheezewhomp appeared.

Did he waddle from the water?

Or crawl from a cave?

Did he swing from a tree?

Or fly from the sky?"

/ / | \

\ ' / /

"No one knows.

From the Wheezewhomp's first night in the
Valley of Strangers, life began to change for
all of the creatures."

/ / \ \

"When his first notes filled their ears, the Wheezewhomp's song transformed the strange creatures' hearts and souls.

Some opened their doors and windows to hear. Some came out of their homes for the first time, turning their eyes and tuning their ears to the sky in wonder."

"One night, the Wheezewhomp sang so joyously that the moonlight seemed to dance through the trees in rhythm to his song.

Everyone felt the energy in the air. We call this night, "The Miracle of Music." For the first time, the song of the Wheezewhomp travelled from our ears to our hearts, and we couldn't contain our own solitary songs any longer."

"The sound built slowly from the depths of our souls. Someone tapped their toes. Another swung his hands in the air. We all began to dance. Then our voices exploded in harmony, melody, and counter melody. The valley overflowed with our music, which travelled over the mountains, across the seas, and throughout the universe."

"The Valley of Strangers was changed
forever that night. We understood each other
for the first time.

We not only sang and danced together, but
we began to truly live together—cooking,
eating, and working together. We transformed
from strangers into friends."

\ | /

"Most importantly, we began to love one another. The Valley of Strangers became The Valley of Love.

We realized that we all did look, smell, and talk strangely, and yet, we were the same.

The Wheezewhomp's song connected us heart to heart and soul to soul. Today, we listen to his song, and we hear each other's songs, as we remember who we are: friends among friends."

/ | \

\\ | /

"Now the Wheezewhomp sings every day at sunset and weeps tears of joy. He shares the peace of his soul with all creatures. Can you hear him? Listen with your heart. Listen to the Wheezewhomp."

The little boy interrupted his mother. "I want to be a Wheezewhomp, Mom. I want to be a Wheezewhomp!"

/ | | \

"Then sing, my little creature. Sing with all your heart. Be the Wheezewhomp."

ABOUT THE AUTHOR

Jules Burke is a dad, a chef, and an author. He loves writing, playing in the kitchen, and sharing snacks with his dog, Elvis. He lives in Austin, Texas with his beautiful wife, Charlotte and their two Wheezewhomps, Max and Ollie.

ABOUT THE ILLUSTRATOR

LeeAnn is a retired middle school art teacher from Gunnison, Colorado. She is inspired by her children, grandchildren, and great grandchildren.

Be the wheezeworms!

♡

LeeAnn

Jules and his dog, Elvis, give cooking lessons on their YouTube channel, Cooking Away the Blues.